BIRDO

To Paul – H.B.
To Sophie – W.A.

First published in 1995

3 5 7 9 10 8 6 4 2

© Text Henrietta Branford 1995
© Illustrations Wayne Anderson 1995

Henrietta Branford and Wayne Anderson have asserted
their right under the Copyright, Designs and Patents Act, 1988,
to be identified as the author and illustrator of this work

First published in the United Kingdom in 1995 by
Hutchinson Children's Books
Random House UK Limited
20 Vauxhall Bridge Road, London SWlV 2SA

Random House Australia (Pty) Limited
20 Alfred Street, Milsons Point, Sydney
New South Wales 2061, Australia

Random House New Zealand Limited
18 Poland Road, Glenfield
Auckland 10, New Zealand

Random House South Africa (Pty) Limited
P0 Box 337, Bergvlei, South Africa

Random House UK Limited Reg. No. 954009

A CIP catalogue record for this book
is available from the British Library

ISBN: 0 09 176239 1

Printed in Hong Kong

Henrietta Branford

Illustrated by
Wayne Anderson

HUTCHINSON
London Sydney Auckland Johannesburg

Long ago and far away, when magic walked the woods under the shining moon, a baby girl fell under a spell. Hard times followed the spell, and sorrow. For it was cast by a witch who wanted the child for a servant.

As soon as Jocasta was big enough
to stir a pot, the witch put her to
work in the kitchen. Dreadful
things she had to cook there: pigs'
feet, and fish with heads on – all
the horrid things that witches love
to eat. Without Birdo, Jocasta
would not have been able to bear
it. He was her one true friend. His
eyes were bright and dark and his
feathers were brown, all except
one, and that was red.

Time passed, and a secret grew in Jocasta's heart. Secrets are hard to keep, and Jocasta told hers to Birdo.

'Birdo,' she whispered, 'I've had a dream about a lovely place. It's all green and golden and if we lived there instead of here, we could be happy ever after.'

'How could we get there, Jocasta?' asked Birdo.

'I by foot and you by wing,' she said.

Jocasta crept towards the door as quietly as silence. But the door creaked, and the witch heard, and she caught Jocasta by the hair.

'Fly away quick, Birdo,' whispered Jocasta, 'and find the lovely place I dreamed of.'

Off went Birdo. But the witch dragged Jocasta upstairs, pushed her into her bedroom, and locked the door. Cold winds rattled the pans in the witch's kitchen and winter sent frost flowers curling over every window. Jocasta thought she'd die of loneliness.

One morning, Jocasta woke up with an odd feeling. Her back was tickling. Tickle and itch, itch and tickle. Jocasta sat up. Two small bumps had grown between her shoulder blades. How they tickled and tormented her! She heard a noise like eggs cracking. She felt a sharp pain, followed by a soft unfurling feeling. Wings!

There came a flutter at the window. Jocasta looked up and there was Birdo, worn, and lorn, and light as air.

'I found happy-ever-after, Jocasta,' he peeped, 'but it's a long way off. Even if you could escape from here, you couldn't walk that far.'

'Then I'll fly,' said Jocasta, and she showed him her wings.

'They're wonderful!' cried Birdo, perching on her finger. His feathers turned to red and gold, and he glowed in her hand like a sunset.

'Let's go at once,' said Jocasta, and Birdo agreed.

'But if we should be parted on the journey,' he said, 'look for me where you least expect to find me. Look, and look hard, and look again, Jocasta.'

Jocasta and Birdo flew away from the witch's house into the mountains, where the wind howls and the glaciers crack like bones.

'Escape from me, would you, Miss Fly-by-Night?' muttered the witch, for there was nothing that she did not see. And she cast her first spell.

'Break friends, break friends,
Never never make friends,
Auntie's spell will bring you home,
And leave Birdo to die alone.'

At once a little man appeared beside Jocasta.

'What are you doing on my mountain?' he asked.

'Resting,' said Jocasta.

'Dying of cold,' said Birdo.

'Come with me,' said the little man, 'and I will give you supper and a warm bed by my fire. I will give you a crown of gold and silver and a necklace of pearls, and you shall be Queen of the Mountain. But leave the bird behind. I hate anything feathery.'

'He would die if I left him,' said Jocasta.

'Maybe,' said the little man. 'But with me for your friend, you won't be needing him. Leave him behind.'

'I will not!' said Jocasta.

The witch ground her teeth, and the little man vanished.

All night Jocasta and Birdo shook and shivered on the mountain, but in the morning they were still alive, and still together. On they flew until they reached a wood. There Birdo gathered sticks and Jocasta lit a fire.

And still the witch watched, and she cast her second spell.

'Come up, Auntie's friend!
Teeth bite, claws rend,
Sweet child and tasty wren,
Feast upon them in your den!'

Into the firelight leapt a bear.

'Who dares burn my wood?' he growled.

'I do,' said Jocasta. 'You have plenty.'

'You took my wood and you shall pay for it,' snarled the bear. 'You shall be my dinner!' Jocasta felt his hot bear's breath on her cheek, but she stood her ground and shook her head.

'I will not!' she said.

'Then give me the wren for a titbit,' said the bear, 'for you cannot escape me otherwise.' He had not seen Jocasta's wings.

'I will not!' said Jocasta. And away she flew, with Birdo by her side.

'Fool bear!' muttered the witch. She ground her teeth, and the bear melted back into the wood.

All that night Jocasta flew, with Birdo by her side, and all the next day, until the setting sun shone up to them from a great bowl of ice. Huge trees stood with their feet in the frozen marsh and the dark path wound away between them. Jocasta lit a fire and lay down.

And still the witch watched, secretly, by magic. 'So, Miss True-Heart,' she hissed, 'still faithful to Little Eyebright? We'll see about that.' And she cast her third spell.

'Feathers red, feathers brown,
Let the bird come tumbling down.
Crack ice, break heart,
Friends and lovers all must part!'

Far out on the lake the ice began to split and splinter, and a dark figure slid towards the shore. Into the ring of firelight stepped the witch. Her black rags flapped in the wind and her face shone like a bone. Fear held Jocasta still as a stone, and Birdo hid.

'Jocasta!' hissed the witch. 'Come here, and let me clip those pretty wings.'

'No,' whispered Jocasta. 'I will not!'

'Then I will come to you. The bird cannot help you. What will you give me, Jocasta, to let you go free?'

'What have I got that you want, Auntie Witch?'
    'I want your one true friend.'
    'Never!'
    'Then you shall be my slave for ever!'
    'Fly, Jocasta!' cried Birdo. 'Now!' And he beat about the
witch's face with his wings to hide Jocasta from her sight.

Away flew Jocasta in the black night, thinking always that Birdo must be just in front of her or just behind. Once she thought she heard him calling her. 'Look for me where you least expect to find me! Look, and look hard, and look again, Jocasta!'

When the long night was over, Jocasta saw soft woods and fields all golden in the morning light.

'We're here!' she called. 'This is the country that I dreamed of, Birdo!'

But Birdo didn't answer. He was nowhere to be seen. Jocasta flew high and low, searching and calling for him, until at last she understood that he had not come with her.

Without Birdo there will be no happy-ever-after, she thought. I will stay here, and wait until he comes.

She built a house for herself, and a nest close by for Birdo. Winter came, and tore at the nest. Snow fell on woods and fields, house and nest, but Birdo did not come.

Spring warmed to summer, woods and fields turned green again, but still he did not come.

    'He will not come now,' sighed Jocasta. 'He will not come ever.' She picked a rose and put it in the tree, in memory of his rose red feathers.

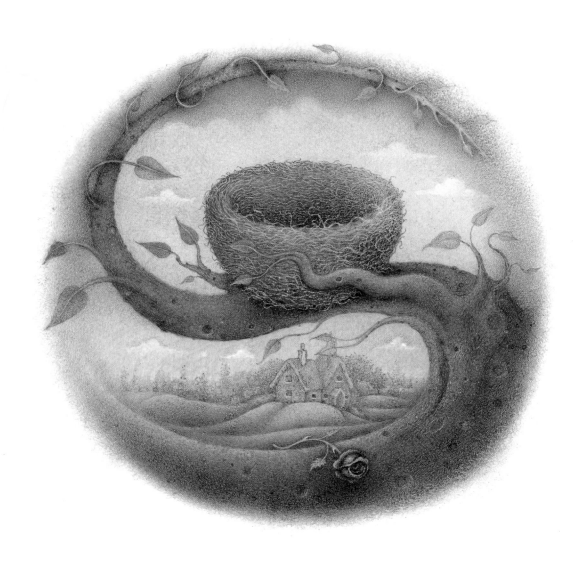

One morning a young man came walking by. At first Jocasta did not see him. She was thinking about Birdo. The young man's hair shone red in the sunlight, and he looked fondly at Jocasta out of his bright dark eyes.

'Who is the rose for?' he asked.

'It's for my love. But he will never see it.'

'Never is a long time,' said the young man. 'Have you forgotten what I told you? Look, and look hard, and look again.'